CW00869304

THIS LITTLE BIRD BOOK
BELONGS TO...

THIS LITTLE BIRD LEARNS
Can't Is Not A Word

Written and Illustrated by Tia K Carrigan

For Boomi's Mrs Mac.

...'that' teacher that
everyone is grateful for.

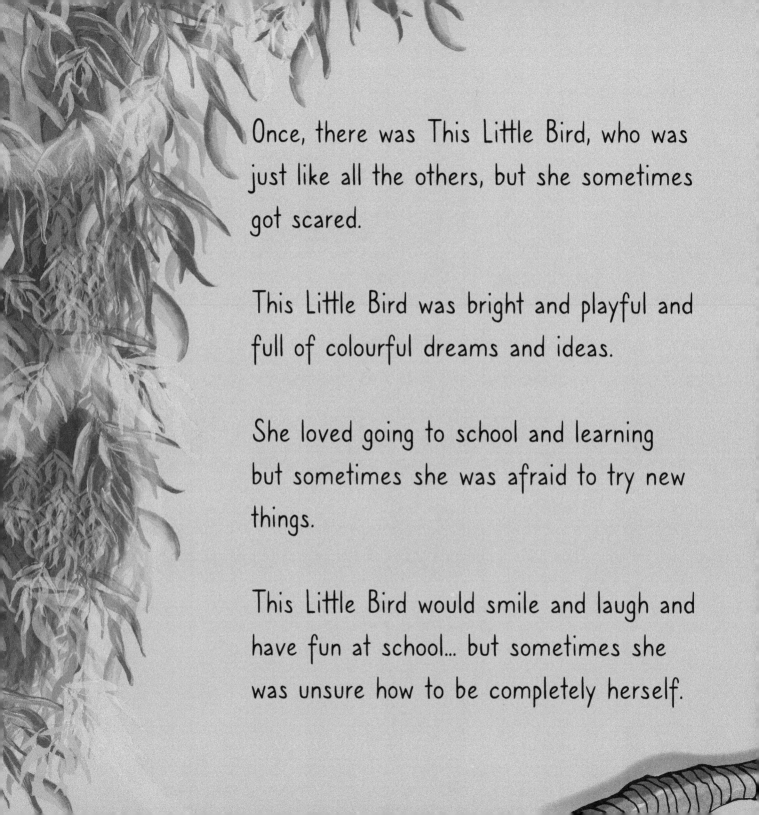

Once, there was This Little Bird, who was just like all the others, but she sometimes got scared.

This Little Bird was bright and playful and full of colourful dreams and ideas.

She loved going to school and learning but sometimes she was afraid to try new things.

This Little Bird would smile and laugh and have fun at school... but sometimes she was unsure how to be completely herself.

Luckily for This Little Bird, she had Mrs Mac for her teacher.

Mrs Mac was as wise as she was happy and cheerful. She always believed her students could do anything they put their mind to.

Whenever This Little Bird felt scared, she would say to herself, "I can't do it".

With a chuckle and a sparkle in her eye, Mrs Mac would remind her everytime:

"There is no such word as can't!"

This Little Bird liked
the idea of being
around new people...
but she says,

"it's too scary to talk to other birds. I can't do it."

Mrs Mac knew This Little Bird was
scared and, with a chuckle and a
sparkle in her eye, she wrapped
her wings around her and said,

"there is no such word as can't.

Be brave and remember, sometimes
the scariest things mean we have
something exciting to learn.

You CAN talk to
other birds."

So, This Little Bird told herself "I CAN"...
and she went....
and she did it...

She made a lovely little friend to laugh
with and share her favourite things.

Now This Little Bird,
says can't is not a word.

This Little Bird wanted to dance how she liked but she was scared of looking silly.

"It's too scary to dance my way in front of everyone. I can't do it."

Mrs Mac knew This Little Bird was scared and, with a chuckle and a sparkle in her eye, she wrapped her wings around her and said,

"there is no such word as can't.

Just be brave, have fun and remember that everyone dances differently.

You CAN dance your way!"

So, This Little Bird told herself "I CAN"...
and she went....
and she did it.

She ended up dancing HER
way, not caring if she looked
silly, and made all the other
little birds smile and clap and
dance along with her.

Now This Little Bird,
says can't is not a word.

This Little Bird loved to be creative in her own way. But it was scary to feel different.

"I want to paint outside the lines, but I feel scared to be creative. I can't do it."

Mrs Mac knew This Little Bird was scared and, with a chuckle and a sparkle in her eye, she wrapped her wings around her and said,

"there is no such word as can't.
The fun happens when you paint outside the lines!

You CAN be creative!"

So, This Little Bird told herself "I CAN"...
and she went...
and she did it...

She covered her paintbrush in all of the
colours and, before she knew it, she had
painted everything around her.

Now This Little Bird,
says can't is not a word.

This Little Bird loved wearing bright colours but she was scared to look different to other little birds.

"I want to wear what I love and express myself but it's scary. I can't do it."

Mrs Mac knew This Little Bird was scared and, with a chuckle and a sparkle in her eye, she wrapped her wings around her and said,

"there is no such word as can't.

Everyone is unique and the world would be so dull if you were like everyone else.

You CAN express yourself!"

So, This Little Bird told herself "I CAN"...

...and she went...

...and she did it.

She wore exactly what she wanted, the brightest colours and patterns and decorated herself with flowers. She couldn't stop smiling.

Now This Little Bird,
says can't is not a word.

This Little Bird loved watching the other birds fly, but she was afraid to try.

"I don't know how to fly, what if I fall? I can't do it."

Mrs Mac knew This Little Bird was scared and, with a chuckle and a sparkle in her eye, she wrapped her wings around her and said,

"there is no such word as can't.
The only way you learn to fly is
to start trying!

You CAN fly!"

So, This Little Bird told herself "I CAN"...

and that she will keep trying...

and so she decided to put on the bright colours she liked to wear...

and she went....

...and she did it!

She FLEW!

Up into the clouds she soared,

feeling beautiful,

wearing bright colours,

splattered with paint,

with her little friends dancing with joy,

and the cheering voice of Mrs Mac filling her ears.

Now This Little Bird sings at the top of her voice,

"I CAN, I CAN, I CAN!"

What will This Little Bird learn next....?

CPSIA information can be obtained
at www.ICGtesting.com
Printed in the USA
LVHW070826121022
730468LV00020B/590

9 780645 585124